Brought to you by

Story With ME

Bringing to life thoughtful stories.

For a smile's sake.

Storywithme.com

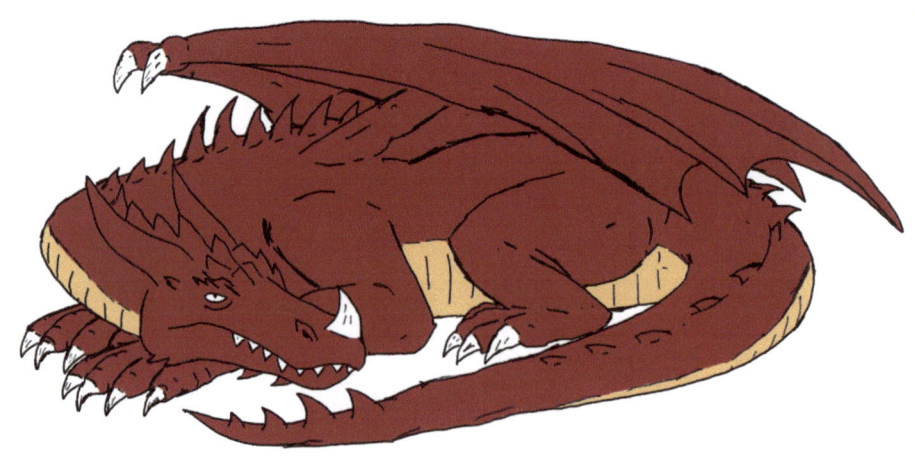

Every good story has a dragon. Without exception.

Don't leave yours asleep.

Searching for...
Invenio

WRITTEN BY
J.J. SCHMIDT

ILLUSTRATED BY
JEREMY WICKHAM

Copyright © 2024 by Jonathon James Schmidt. All rights reserved. No part of this book may be reproduced, stored, or transmitted in any form or by any means with the prior written permission of the publisher, except in the case of brief quotations embodied in articles and reviews.

ISBN 978-1-963935-01-1

This is a work of fiction. Names, characters, places, and events are a fictional product of the author's imagination or are used fictitiously. Any resemblance to actual persons, living or dead, events, or locales is entirely coincidental.

Published by Story With Me.
Storywithme.com

It is a beautiful gift to be here.

For Lauren, Owen, Evan, Catherine, Frankie, Bea and Peter. Thank you for being ours.

Preface

This took me twenty years to finish. I intend that to be neither an impressive nor mortifying fact, as this story has been on a journey far longer than the pages you see. It was started by a boy who did not know what he wanted to do with his life and was finished by a father who wanted to tell his boys that that's entirely okay. I began this all those years ago with the certainty that it was the makings of the next epic fantasy trilogy. Really. The dozens of pages you see before you were originally designed to be hundreds, if not thousands. It took me approximately one month and one hundred pages of writing to have equal certainty that I was out of my mind. What stood between me and the next masterpiece was patience, persistence, and talent. So close.

    Those hundred pages sat and waited, aging less like fine wine and more like a cedar fence—clearly aging, but something about it was oddly functional (a glowing review, I know. Refer to the previous paragraph). Fast forward to May of 2020, in a hospital parking lot, as I sat idle waiting for my 9-month pregnant wife to finish a non-stress test (oh, the irony of this test's name. Though I assure you upfront all went well, and this story was not born out of any tragic events). I happened upon a "Freakonomics Radio" podcast centered on Kevin Kelly's "68 Bits of Unsolicited Advice"—both entirely worth your time and full of brilliant wisdom. "Hey, that seems pretty easy, and I should do that too," is what I thought, and how I imagine most people begin when they are about to be in way over their heads.

So, over the proceeding hour, I frantically cobbled together barely coherent, though literate, life lessons of my own in the form of a note to my unborn child. I was quite pleased. It wasn't Kevin Kelly-worthy, but I found it therapeutic, fulfilling, and a helpful reminder of the compass I use toward my own journey. But the themes from it were oddly familiar. As if I had written it all before. Because I had. Barely baked and only half-understood, but I had constructed it in the form of what was to be the next great fantasy trilogy years prior (again, if it wasn't for that lack of talent…). Never one to toss out good wood, I tore up the aging cedar fence I called my fantasy novel and redesigned it into what you see before you today.

What you'll find next is the intro to the note I wrote to my son that day. For a story that has no beginning, this note serves as the extrinsic opening to Invenio…

Your mother was due 6 days ago. You're a procrastinator, I get it. I used to be like that too, though after 36 years of life, I've matured into "just in time planning" and working "Agile" – these are all traits you'll learn in the business world to make your procrastination sound really fancy. As the great Mark Twain once said, "Never put off till tomorrow what you can do the day after tomorrow." If you've never heard of him before reading this, then I've already failed you, so please put this down now and Google him (if that's still a thing?)

As I sit here in the hospital parking lot while your mother has a "nonstress test" checkup, I am reflecting upon the fact that this, among many other things, will be my responsibility to teach you. The question you should now be asking yourself is – why is he sitting in the hospital parking lot while Mom is having a test? (At least, let me hope you are asking yourself this instead of assuming this is a trait you'd expect out of me). Well, you should know that we are in the middle of the Covid-19 pandemic and seeing as you're lucky enough to be born in the thick of it, I am not allowed in the hospital. Do not pity me. Instead, please pity your poor mother who has carried you for 9 months and now the only things that fit her are my largest pajama pants, whose elastic has broken – and this is how you repay her, by taking your sweet, sweet time. (Please get used to this guilt trip – as we get older this is a tendency that will only get worse, and we have no control over it).

I am getting sidetracked. Let me come back around to the point – 36 years on this earth, I've navigated through a few of the tricky points of life: schooling, career, relationships, etc., etc. (Feel free to use "etc., etc." as a replacement when you know there should be more substance but are drawing a blank). During this time, I feel I've mustered up some knowledge balls of life experience that I feel compelled to present to you (FYI, the unintentional awkward things I say pale in comparison to your mother, best to just give it an eye roll here and move forward). But here it goes... from a nervous, anxious, and wonderfully excited father to his unborn son...

Searching for...
Invenio

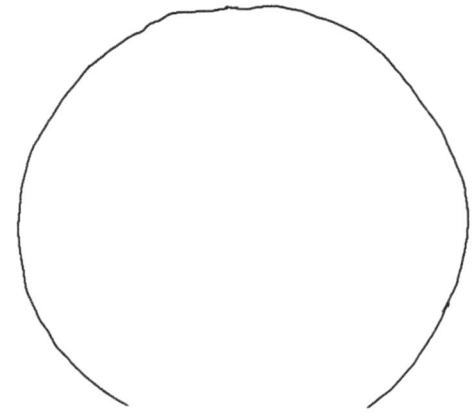

Part 1

Wake. Eat. Work. Sleep.

The first thing you must know is that I am unreliable when it comes to details. For this story and in my world, details do not matter. Or maybe I just do not care. Or perhaps there is no difference? I do not presume to know.

The second thing is that there is no beginning, at least not one that is of any consequence to you. Just details.

Now that we are on the same page, I will start in the middle.

There once was a place that had 200 billion galaxies. In one of those galaxies there were 100 billion planets. On one of those planets there were 8 billion people. Of those people there was a boy.

The Boy was aged the number of years you would expect, doing all the things a boy does, and learning things not at all unexpected.

"What will you do now?" The One Who Teaches asked.

The Boy did not know, and he frowned.

"It is time to do things with all the many great things you've learned here," The One Who Teaches responded assuredly.

The Boy was not assured.

"Well, we've taught you everything there is. So now you must go do things that are of great importance. I hope you find Invenio. It is of course the most important thing." are the last words The One Who Teaches left for The Boy.

Now, when I say do not worry about this detail yet, you will have to trust me. Do you trust me? You know full well how I am with details… but, of course, you have no choice.

At least not yet.

As was expected, The Boy had been sent off to a world to live a life designed at that place with those teachers who had helped with all those things—things he hadn't been so sure of then and was less sure of now. But luckily, they were just details.

So he went back home to The Place of Little Things. They did all sorts of things there. Commendable things. Little things that made other little things happen and then more little things after that. He was qualified to do little things now since he had done things with the teachers who had taught him the things he wasn't so sure of. It was quite commendable.

For days ... or was it months? It could have been years if it were not for his lack of aging during this commendable time. Wake. Eat. Work. Sleep. Repeat. It was the way. And it seemed very important to everyone that it be important to him to do very unimportant things. Certainly, this wasn't Invenio? That is a silly question for me to ask you, knowing that I just asked you not to worry about this detail.

As The Boy sat down at his desk to work on all the things, he noticed his fine acquaintance, The One Who Works, looking quite disgruntled next to him.

The One Who Works noticed The Boy notice him but pretended not to notice. "Ughhhh!" The One Who Works sighed dramatically.

Now, when I tell you The Boy did not check on The One Who Works at that given moment, do not be too harsh in your judgment. This is to be expected at The Place Of Little Things. They sigh quite often. Silently and loudly. Aggressively and politely. In my world, it does not get you very far. Is it different from yours? I doubt it, but I do not want to presume.

"I must get to Invenio!" The One Who Works exclaimed and sighed at no one in particular but also particularly at The Boy.

Now, when I tell you The Boy still did not check on The One Who Works at that given moment, I acknowledge that your harsh judgments are getting closer to becoming valid. But remember, The Boy was only of the age that was determined by your expectations in the beginning. He still had quite a bit of aging to do ... most likely.

Despite the indifference to his sighing, The One Who Works was undeterred, if not more motivated to sigh, for this is the way of people who often sigh.

"You know what I'm talking about, right?" The One Who Works asked.

No one did.

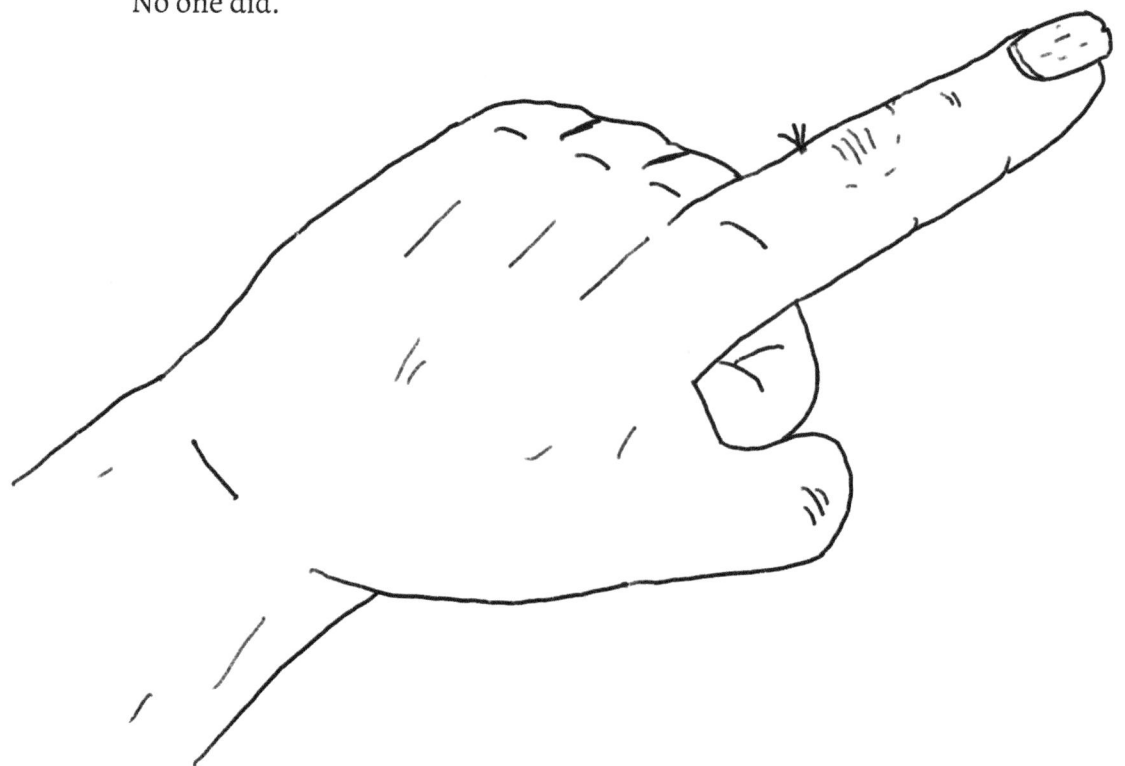

"There!" The One Who Works said, pointing out of the window toward the sky. "You see it?"

Far off in the distance, there was a land in the sky.

"That's where The Big People are! Doing all the big things!" The One Who Works sighed. "That's where I'm going."

The Boy thought about that while The One Who Works continued to sigh. Little things were commendable, but big things seemed exciting. Would you agree? The Boy was not so sure.

The One Who Works continued to sigh for a good long while—40 or maybe 50 years? He had been sighing long before The Boy came, and he did so long after he left. I think The One Who Works may have mistaken sighing for something other than what it is. But I do not presume to know.

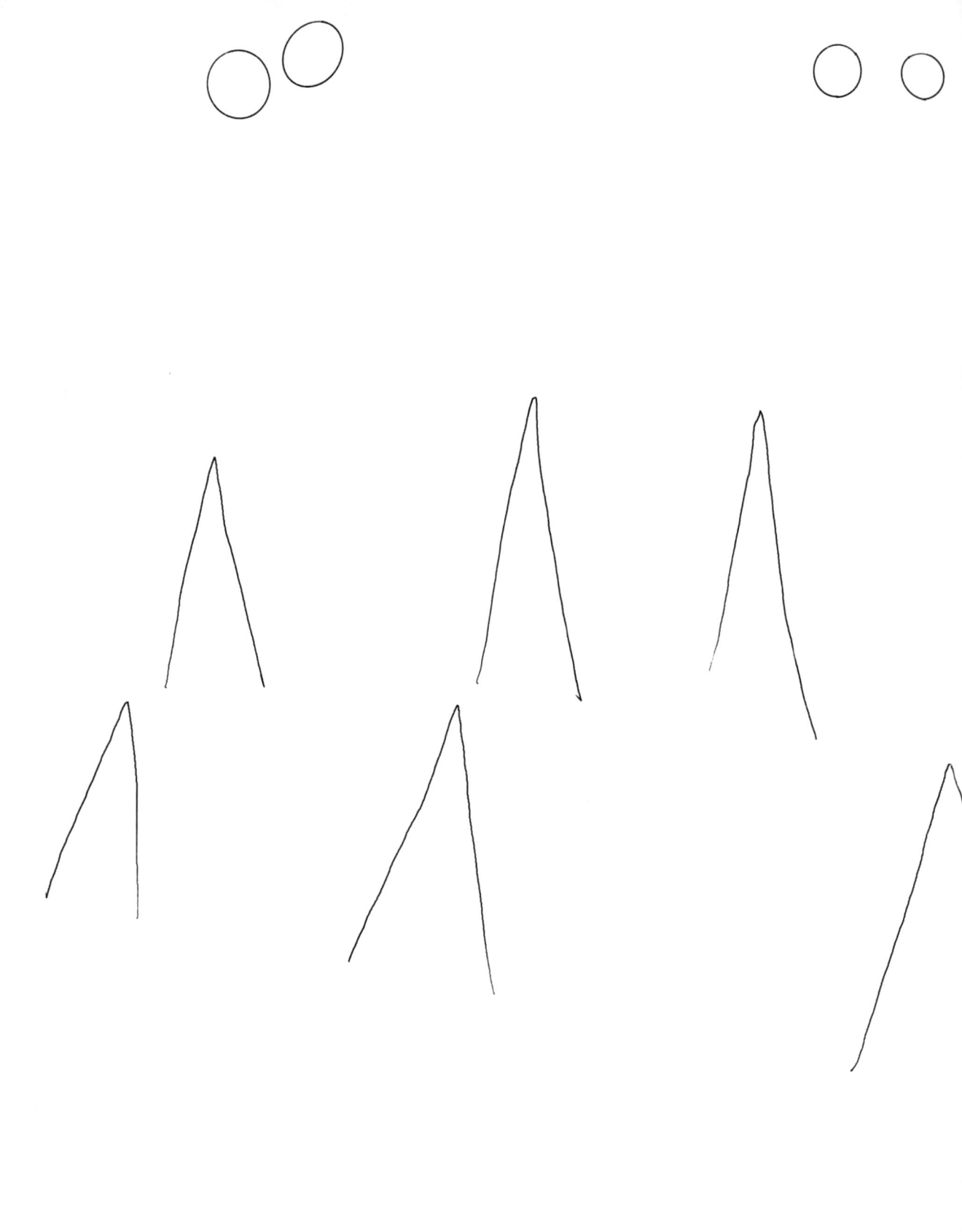

Part 2

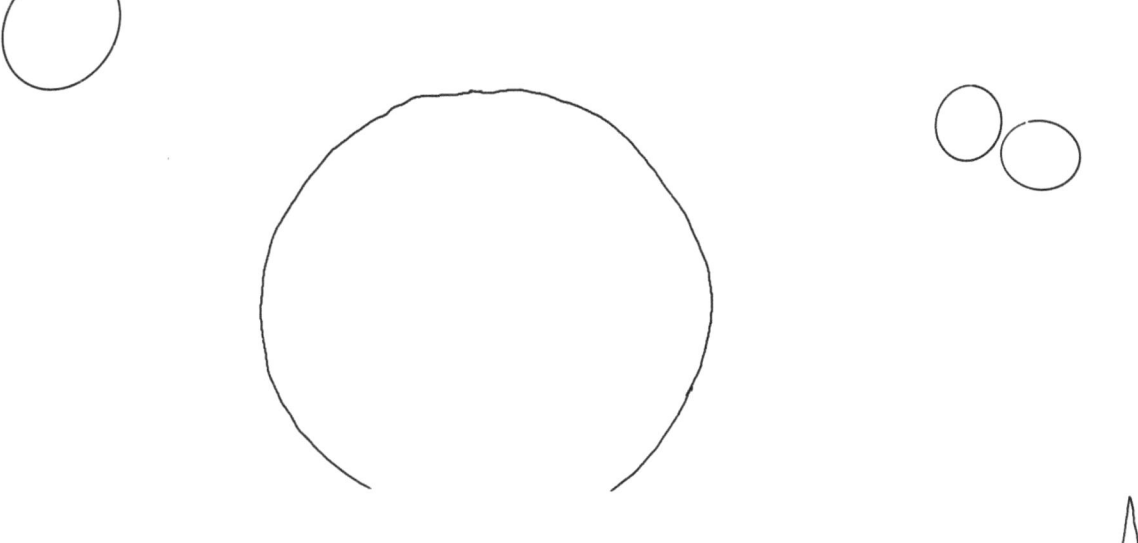

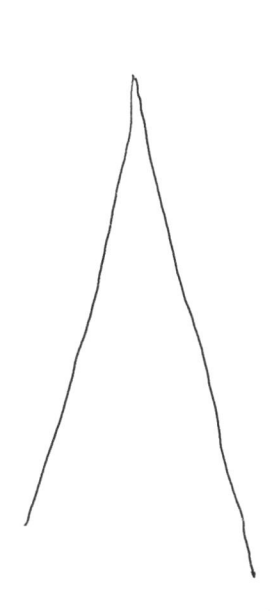

If Only He'd Asked a Single Question.

Sometime later, The Boy was walking from place to place when he encountered a strange-looking little ship and an even stranger-looking individual standing next to it.

"Aha! You look like you are in need of a ride!" said The One Who Adventures. "I am off to Invenio. Will you be joining?"

What luck!

The Boy, of course, joined The One Who Adventures. Afterall, how could he not? In my world it is not advisable to jump onto odd little ships with odd little people. However, I never said they were strangers; that was just you assuming, I'd assume. These are just details afterall.

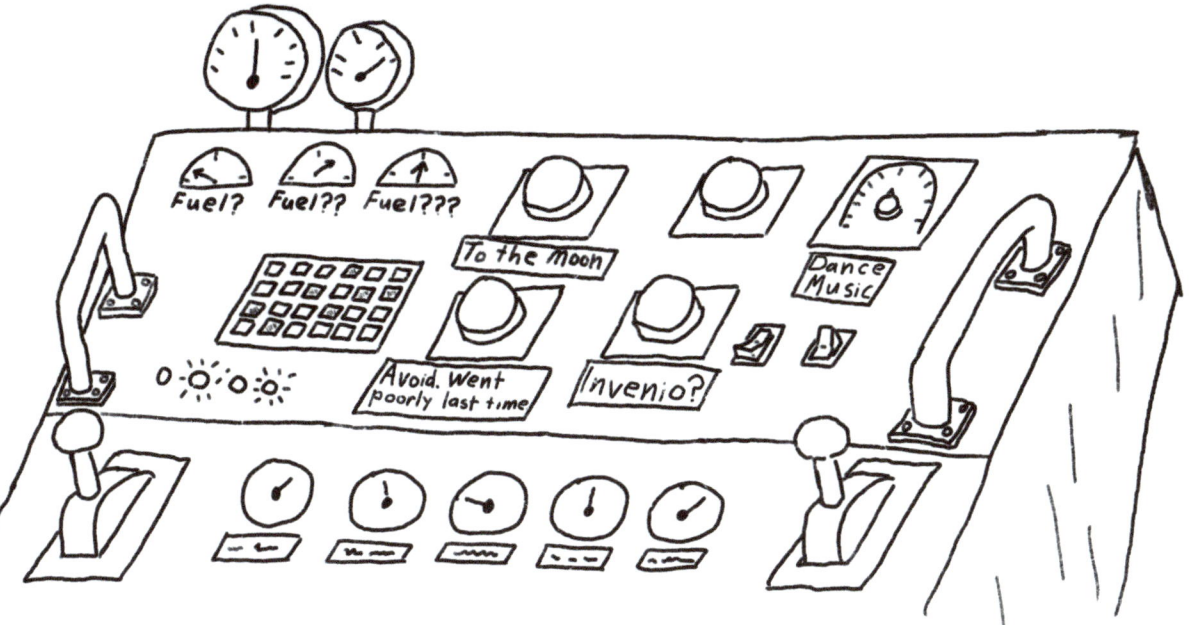

Levers were pushed, buttons were pulled, and the ship slowly rose from the ground. What fueled the ship was quite a mystery, but The One Who Adventures was quite confident so that was reassuring.

"I assure you I know where Invenio is," The One Who Adventures declared, unprompted. "I've been to a great many places and done a great many things. I can assure you that I have great control of this ship and plenty of fuel to reach Invenio."

The more The One Who Adventures gave assurances, the less reassured The Boy felt. In fact, The One Who Adventures seemed to have no control over the ship at all. It jumped to great heights and sank to steep lows unforgivingly. The Boy was beginning to fear they would crash, but you would never know it looking at The One Who Adventures.

"I assure you I have full control. I've been to Invenio, you see. I have it all quite figured out. And I assure you there's plenty of fuel."

The Boy was now panicking and felt an urgent need to check on the fuel, if only he knew what this ship was running on. He felt quite a bit of regret for not asking more questions before boarding. Or any questions, really. If only he'd asked a single question!

I do not know how long they were up there, or how long it took them to come to after the crash. These are but minor details. But upon waking, The One Who Adventures exclaimed without hesitation, "Invenio is just up ahead!" and The Boy felt reassured once again.

Some lessons are not learned the first time.

"Do not worry about my ship! I had full control and plenty of fuel. I've been to Invenio countless times," The One Who Adventures said.

Some lessons are never learned.

The boy departed, for now, while The One Who Adventures picked up the pieces of his ship of which he had full control. The Boy walked for only a short while before he came upon two buildings. One was circular and the other triangular, but otherwise, they looked remarkably similar in terms of craftsmanship and structure. Standing outside were two remarkably similar people engaged in passionate debate over what must have been remarkably important things.

As The Boy approached, the person near the triangular structure stopped the intense debate and scurried toward him in a great hurry. "You there! Are you new here? I've never seen your face before. This is The Place of Only Right and Wrong. Let me introduce myself. I am The One Who is Right. I must insist you join my side as I'm sure I do not need to explain to you that triangular is how everything must be. Anything that is otherwise is wrong! Very wrong! Can I count on your support?"

At that very moment, the second person scurried even quicker to join the conversation. "Hey, newcomer! I am sorry that you're being bothered by this person. Let me introduce myself. I am The One Who is Correct. I know you realize how everything must be circular and that anything else would be very wrong. That's plain to see by anyone with sense. Can I count on your support?"

Now, let me take a moment to tell you that in The Boy's world there were a great many objects and shapes. There were so many that it was impossible to know them all or what they meant. It brought him a moment of great comfort to know that maybe things came in just triangles or circles and everything else was wrong. Are things so simple in your world? I'd imagine not, but I do not want to presume.

The Boy listened as The One Who is Right argued with The One Who is Correct for quite some time. A long time even. Or maybe forever.

"Squabble squabble squabble, triangles!" screamed The One Who is Right.
"Squabble, squabble, squabble, circles!" The One Who is Correct screamed louder.
"Triangles, squabble, squabble, squabble!" The One Who is Right yelped even louder.
"Circles, squabble, squabble, squabble!" The One Who is Correct yelped even louder than that.

As The Boy contemplated how remarkably alike and remarkably silly it all sounded, people started pouring out of the buildings on both sides—dozens and dozens of people, if not millions.

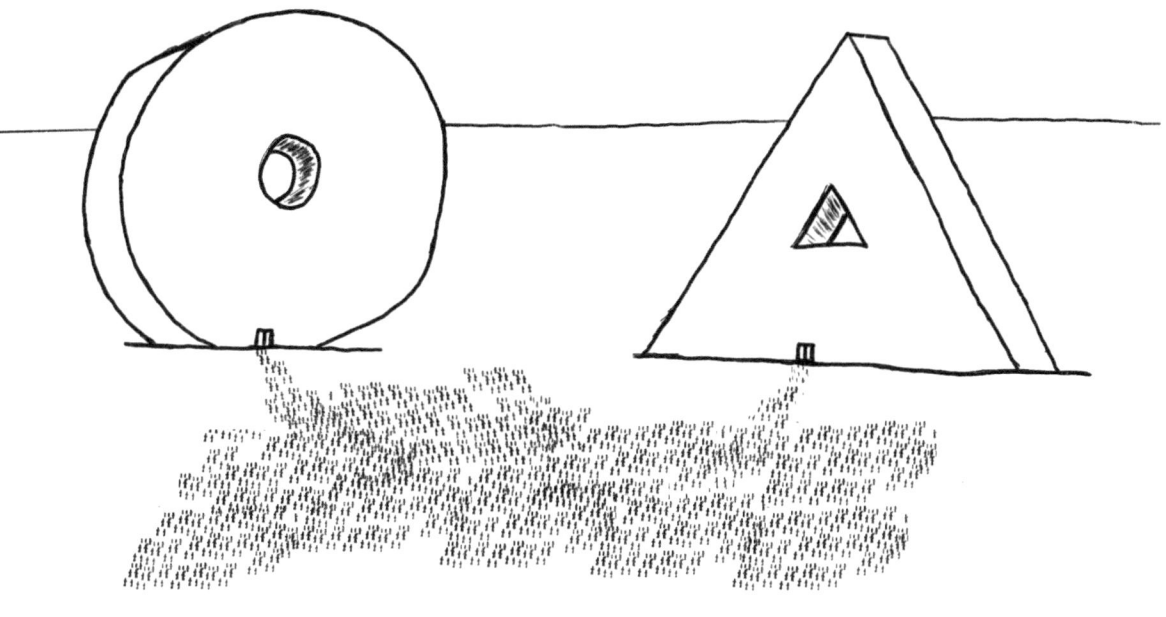

"Triangles!" one side yelled.
"Circles!" the other side yelled back.

The One Who Is Right, and The One Who is Correct both looked quite satisfied.

What precisely both sides were arguing about at that precise moment on that precise day did not matter. The answers were always the same in a world with just triangles and circles. So, the crowd stopped to stare at The Boy while awaiting his decision, and it was at that moment that he decided to move onward. Maybe he would return later. He was not sure. Maybe he would come back with a cone.

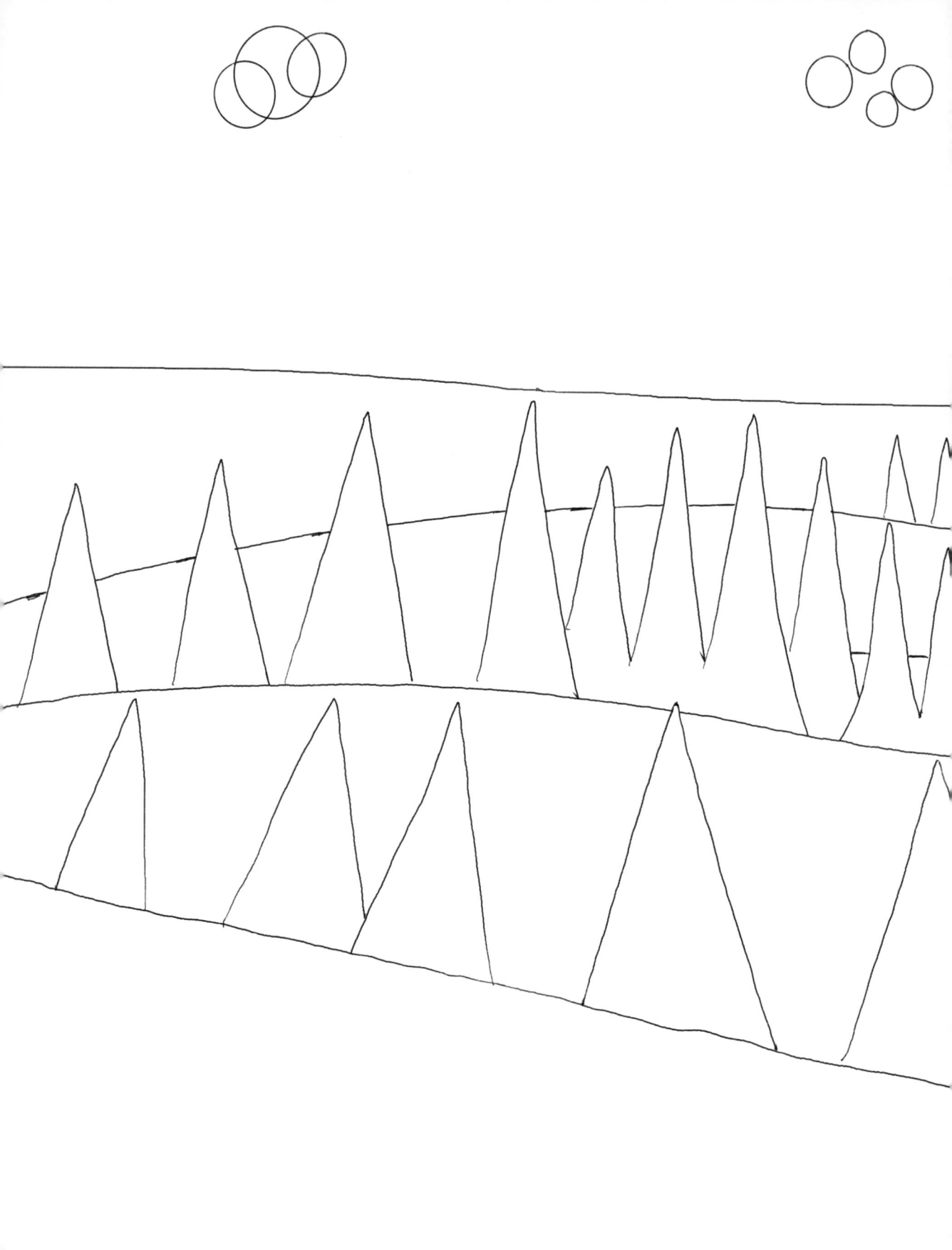

Part 3
Every Good Story Has a Dragon.
Without Exception.

For a short time, The Boy wandered. He walked to this place, then that place, and then back to this place. Invenio was starting to feel very far-off; in fact, he was not sure he'd ever known the way at all. And these places he walked to and from failed to provide greater clarity.

He eventually walked to another place, and there it was—The Dragon. It was a beautiful force of nature, something he had never encountered before. Does it surprise you that there are dragons in this world? Well, do not be silly! Every good story has a dragon. Without exception.

The Boy did not know how to approach it. And he was not much for words. Did you notice that? But The Dragon was not much for waiting and did not care about The Boy's words or the lack thereof. The creature lurched forward and flexed its magnitude. It is difficult for me to say how large The Dragon was, as The Boy is the only one who really knows. The Dragon was somewhere in the range of one hundred to infinity times The Boy's size. As The Dragon spread its wings out and around The Boy, it completely engulfed him.

There he was with a dragon, relaxed and content. I think he knew this was not Invenio, but I assure you that when you are engulfed by a dragon, not much else matters. Do my assurances reassure you? I hope not, as we've already been over that.

The Boy experienced a great many new things with The Dragon. They flew to great heights and explored many worlds. The Boy was in awe of the fire The Dragon could generate from a simple breath. Sure, a few villages were burned down. But that's what happens when you're with a dragon. Right? It was certainly something that could not be stopped. Anyway, that is how The Boy felt, at least for a while.

Then one day, as they soared through the sky at great speed, The Dragon decided that it was done with The Boy and released him from its wings. The Boy went into free fall. You would think he would be very scared while falling from such a great height. On the contrary, he was only woeful and spiteful toward The Dragon. Could it not have set him down gently on the ground? Or at least given him a parachute? But those are silly expectations when you're dealing with a beautiful force such as a dragon. Anyone else would have pointed this out very clearly, but it is quite different when you are the one engulfed.

When The Boy hit the ground, it hurt. And he lay there for a great long while. I think it is okay to lie down in a place for some time when you fall that hard. Do you agree? One can at least lie down long enough to appreciate they are no longer contributing to the fires.

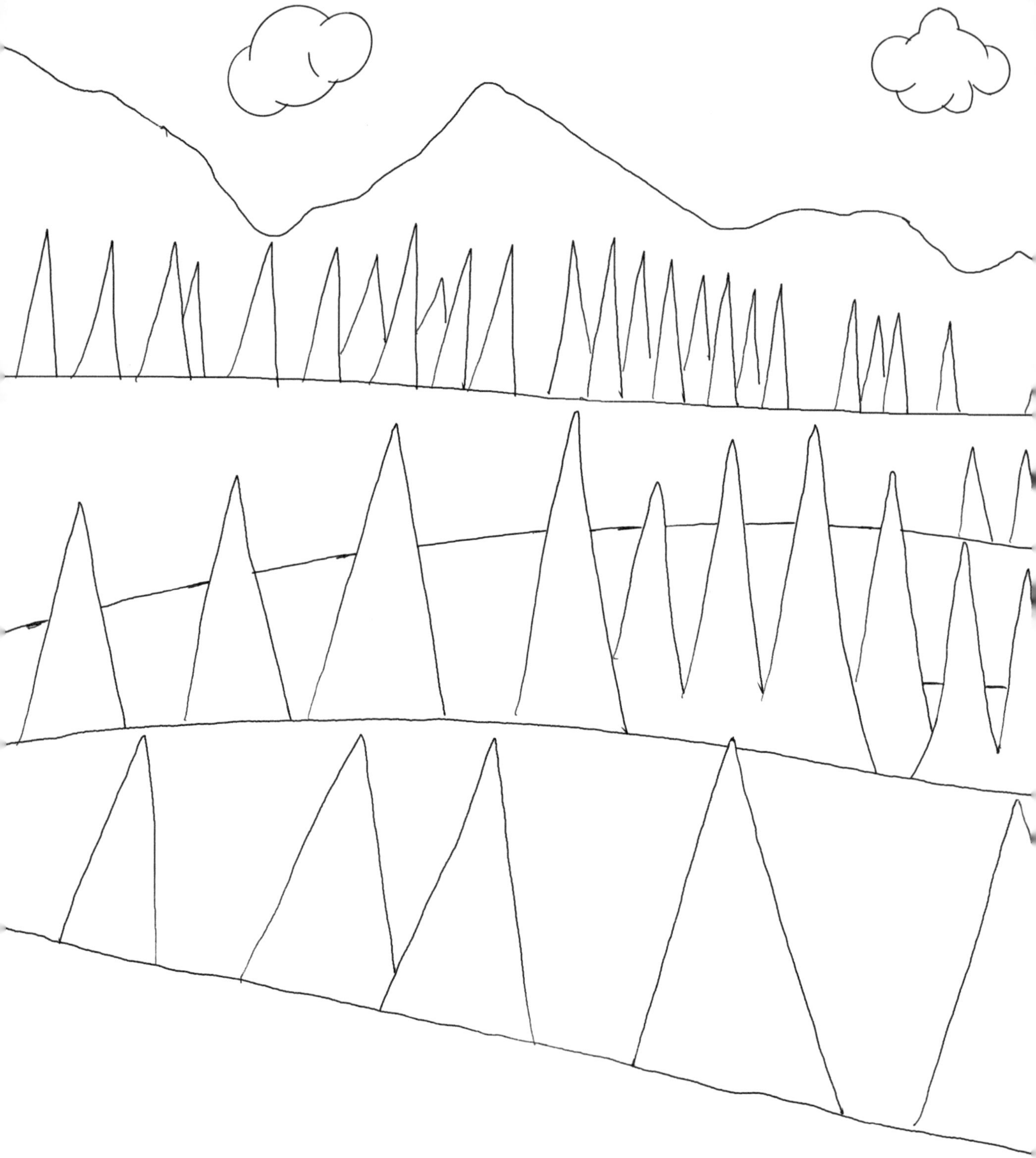

Part 4

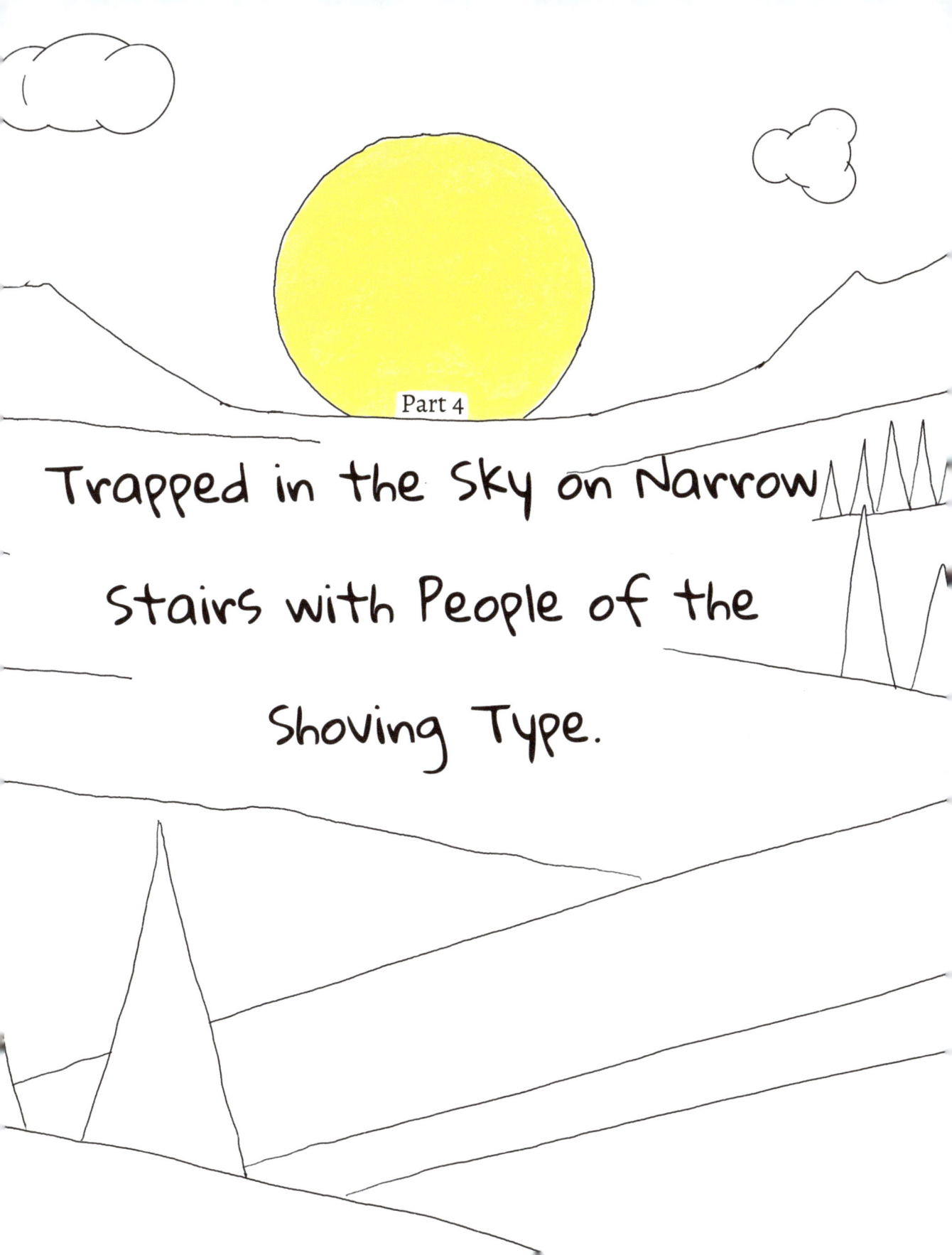

Trapped in the Sky on Narrow Stairs with People of the Shoving Type.

When The Boy finally got up, he found that he was right next to a large set of stairs. When he looked up, he could see it was leading to a land in the sky. It was the same land that The One That Works had always dreamed of getting to—The Land of Big People. Was it Invenio?

The Boy was rejuvenated. Focused. Fueled. Fueled with what? It is hard to say. Maybe the same fuel The One Who Adventures used? I do not think so, and few, if any, questions were asked.

The first few steps were easy. There was plenty of room for all who wanted to go up. But it did not stay that way for long. As he got higher, the stairs began to get narrower and it was starting to get crowded. Every so often, a door would block the way, and he could not progress to the next step until it opened. He did not know how these doors were controlled, or why some doors did not seem to open for everyone, but he did not have to wait long for most.

The stairs grew even narrower, and that's when the others started shoving each other. After all, it was the easiest way to proceed. The Boy started to shove as well, for it was the way. And as long as it was the way, it was okay. Would you agree? No, of course not, but then again, we are not trapped in the sky on narrow stairs with people of the shoving type.

When the first few people fell off the side of the stairs, it was slightly startling. But this did not bother most; in fact, it seemed to have been expected. Soon, it became routine. It was how you climbed fast that was, of course, the most important thing in this world. The Boy became quite good at climbing over people. Sometimes, he would pin them down to walk over them, then sidestep others. To his credit, he did his best to not push anyone off. Do you give him credit for this? For being less worse than the worst? I don't suppose so …

I do not know how long it took or how many people had to fall before The Boy reached the final door at the very top. When it opened, The Big Person was there and looked down at all those who had made it to the final door. With very little thought, The Big Person grabbed The Boy, swiftly brushed everyone else off the steps, and closed the door. What luck!

"Welcome to The Place of Very, Very, Very Big Things," The Big Person said. "You are now one of us. All the things we do here are the biggest, most important things. We are the biggest people around. Much bigger than all those small people down there. So embarrassingly small!" The Big Person laughed knowingly.

The Big Person appeared very big to The Boy indeed. He had finally found Invenio, and that was reassuring. Would you agree? No, of course not.

The Big Person walked him through the land. They had everything there, anything a person could want or imagine. Is there something big that you've ever imagined having? Well, yes, they had that too. And they soaked in all the light here. They were so high up that nothing could block the light shining on this land.

"We control all the doors, you know." The Big Person said and laughed knowingly.

This confused The Boy. He had come across a great many doors, and he had been able to open or close most himself. Did The Big Person think the doors on the stairs up were the only ones?

"We only let the good ones through. We control it all. Every door."

The Boy did not like that.

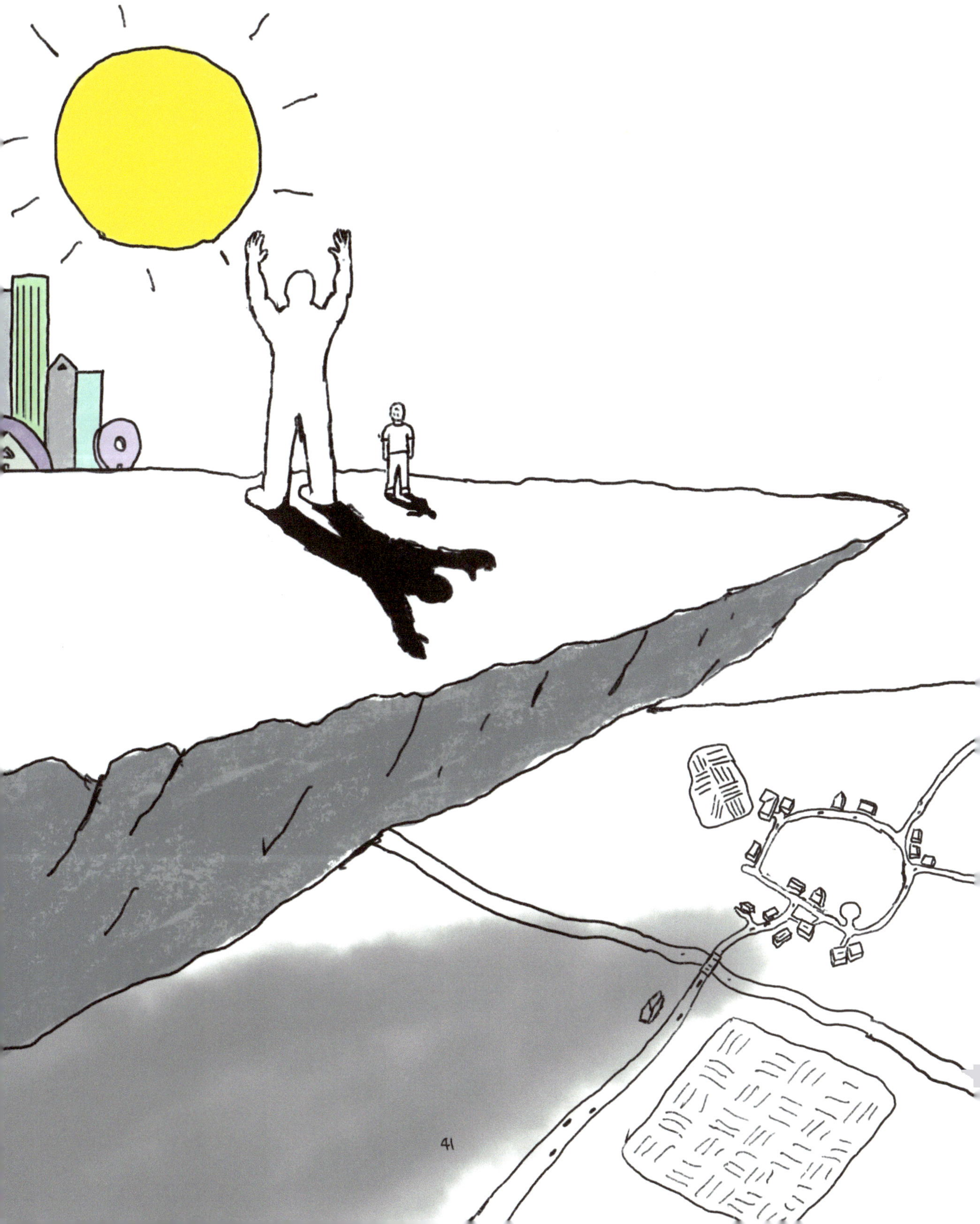

"Come over here! Let me show you all the big things we do." The Big Person grabbed a bucket of bricks, led them to the edge of the land, and attached a brick to the end with great ease. "Here, you try," The Big Person said as he handed The Boy a brick and then laughed knowingly.

The Boy approached the edge, placed the brick lightly, and it extended the land that much further. It was then that he noticed the new shadow cast. His newly placed brick now blocked some light, preventing it from making it down to the land below.

"Ah, you did a very big thing there! And it's so easy from up here, isn't it? So easy but so big and important," The Big Person said with glee.

This is when The Boy noticed that all the big people were effortlessly extending the land, slowly shielding more and more of the light and preventing it from reaching the people below. He did not understand why. They already had everything up here. Was it not enough? Despite having that thing you imagined?

The Boy thought about the people down below and the people on the stairs—the ones that fell, the ones that were climbed over, and the ones stuck behind doors. The Boy was done placing bricks.

43

The Big Person chuckled. Quite knowingly, but not assuredly.

"You think you have a choice up in this place? I control it all. The doors, the bricks, the shadows. This story. Your story. I control that, too!"

The Boy did not like that. I did not like that. I do not

Excuse me. I am in the middle of narrating

This was not very commendable. Rude, even.

"Do you think any of that matters to me? Or up here?" The Big Person boasted. "You are nothing. Your story is nothing. What we do up here is all that matters. You can join or you can be in our shadow."

With that, The Big Person seemed to grow in even larger stature to The Boy. So big that the sunlight, just moments ago plentiful, became scarcely visible.

"I control more than you even comprehend. The circles. The triangles. The colors."

The Big Person held a brick up in the air and blocked the sun fully.

Then the shadows came. Suffocating. Was this all there was? This was Invenio?

But this was not the end, and it was not Invenio. The shadows became lighter as he moved back toward the stairs. But it was hard. The things up here were so big and plentiful, which was reassuring. And The Big Person had a gravitational pull that could not be explained. So hard to move, but he continued. To The Boy's surprise, The Big Person did not stop him from going back down the stairs. In fact, he could not. No doors were there to block his way.

It was easy to move from there. The stairs were wide, and there was no shoving. Interestingly, most people he encountered going down seemed to be quite relieved.

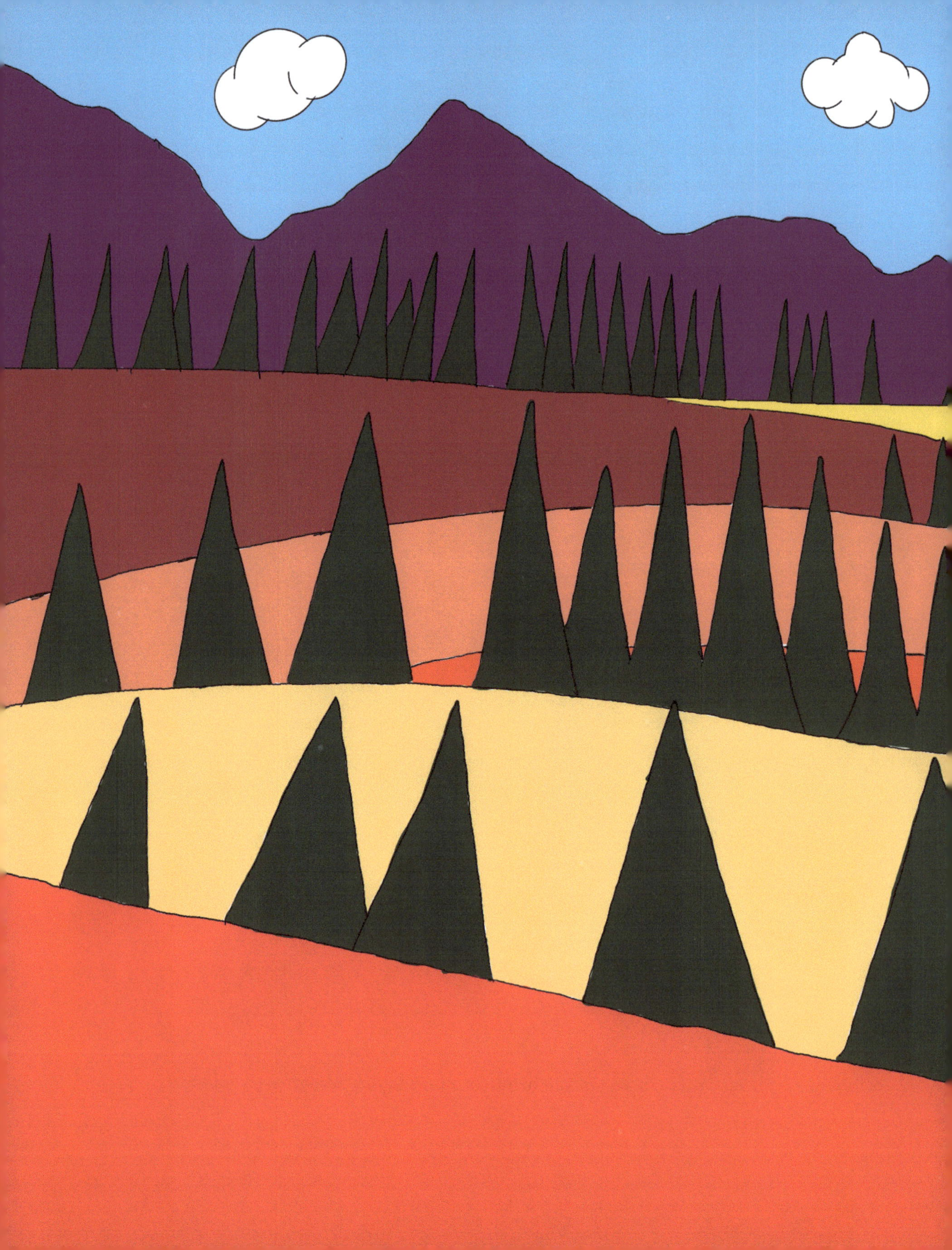

Part 5

Invenio.

The Boy reached the bottom, and he was lost. Did Invenio even exist? He lay down and did not move for quite some time. That is when I found him.

"Did you not find what you were looking for up there?" I asked him. "No, of course, you did not," I responded to myself.

I pride myself on understanding the answers to my own questions. Had you noticed? Yes, of course, you did.

"Lying down is good. It gives you the opportunity to get back up. It is time to get back up now," I said to The Boy. "Follow me."

Now, in my world, it is not advisable to follow a stranger to an undisclosed location. I won't bother asking if it is the same in yours. But, of course, I am far from a stranger.

We did not walk for long; in fact, our destination was always close. We arrived at a place that you may consider quite small, and you may consider the things inside it smaller still. Tiny even. You would be wrong though. Very wrong. But that's only because I skipped the beginning, so I do not blame you. Maybe that's the way of most small things?

A door stood in our path. The Boy approached it cautiously, but as he pushed it opened with ease.

"You looked surprised," I said. "Do not be, this door opens for those that try. It is the way of most doors, you see."

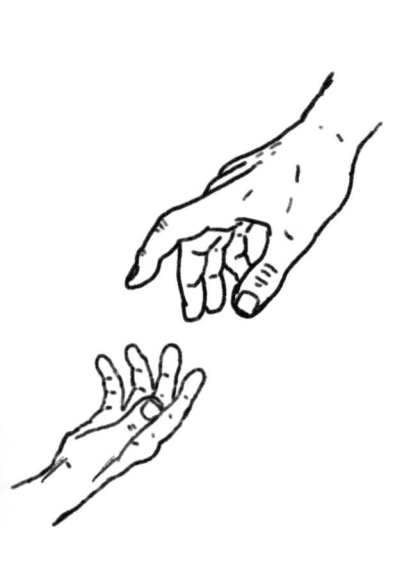

We passed through a corridor and stepped into an open room. The walls were mostly bare but for a few items of unique shapes, the kind you may consider worthless. But you'd be even more wrong than earlier. Wildly wrong. I am very particular about how I line my walls. It took me quite a bit of practice to not fill my walls with countless knick-knacks. Decades and decades of practice. I will continue practicing until the walls are gone.

In the center of the room were three flowers. Light beamed in through the open ceiling and shone upon them. You might think these three flowers are fairly common and can be found anywhere. I cannot stress how wrong you would be on this point. Inconceivably wrong. These are the only flowers in this room and within these walls. They are the most important things.

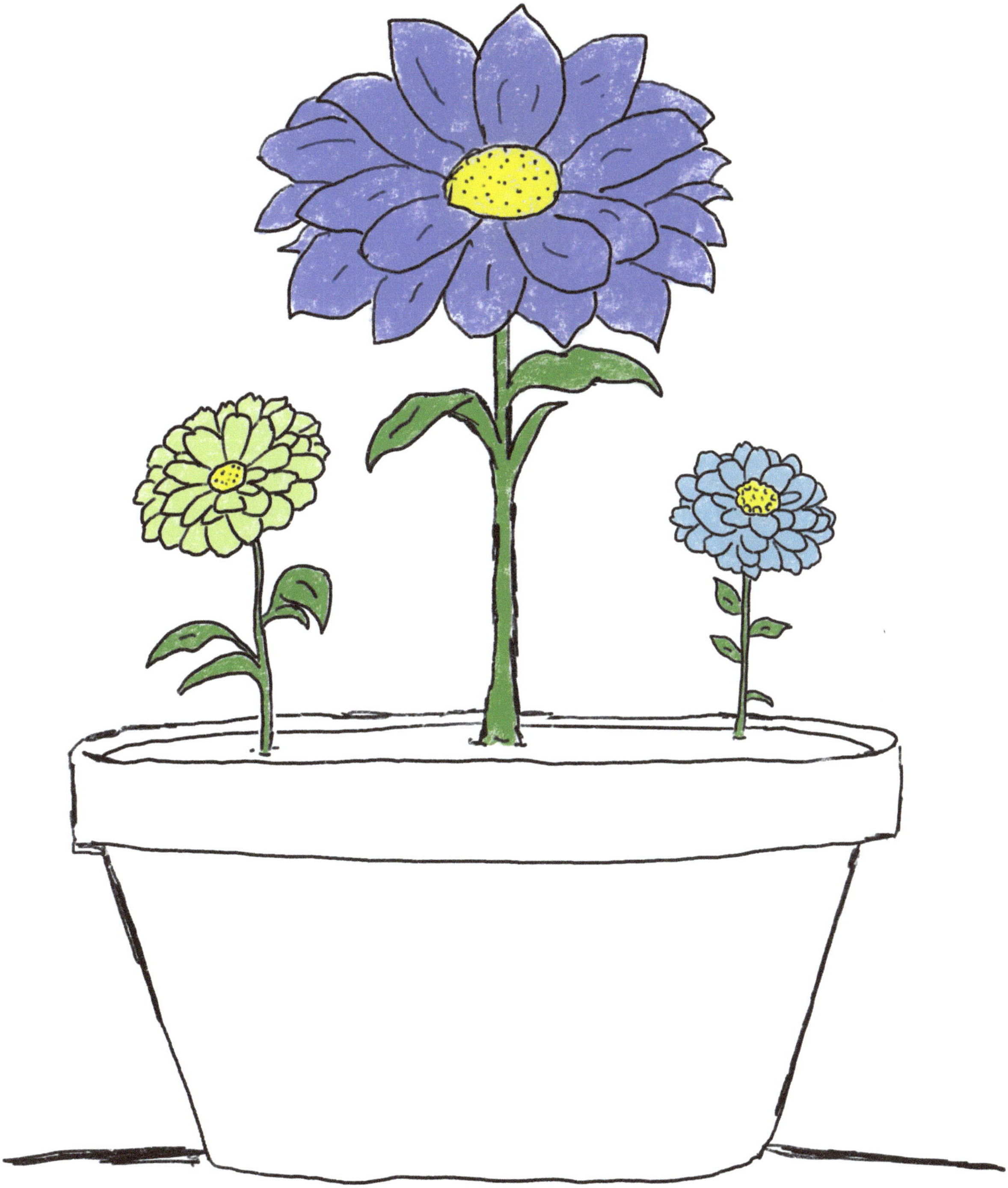

"Is this Invenio?" I asked The Boy.

The Boy was surprised by the question. Maybe it had not occurred to him that the answer was entirely his to decide? The Boy thought about all the shapes, dragons, people, and places he had visited ... he was not so sure. I beamed with pride and chuckled, maybe even a bit knowingly.

"I do not have any grand reassurances for you. There are a great many things to be encountered in this world. More stairs, small things, and big things. I've been engulfed more times than I care to share and caught in shadows from above."

The Boy stared up at the open sky nervously.

"Ah, do not be concerned. I've spent much time climbing stairs to get out of The Big People's shadows, and it used to be very important to me to have big things within these walls. This was before I had my flowers. Just details. If shadows come, I will move with my flowers. The shadows only stay for as long as we allow. It is entirely up to us, you see?"

The Boy pondered this for a while.

"Bah, this is getting dangerously close to a reassurance! I assure you I have none," I said assuredly. "You are always welcome here while you search. And keep searching. It is a beautiful gift."

The Boy thought for a while longer. It is helpful to stop and think, I think.

"What will you do now?" I asked. The Boy did not know, and he smiled.

The third thing you must know is that there is no ending or, at least, not one that has been written yet. It is not for me to tell.

The last thing ... no, that would be too much detail. I will leave that for you to discover.

Searching for...

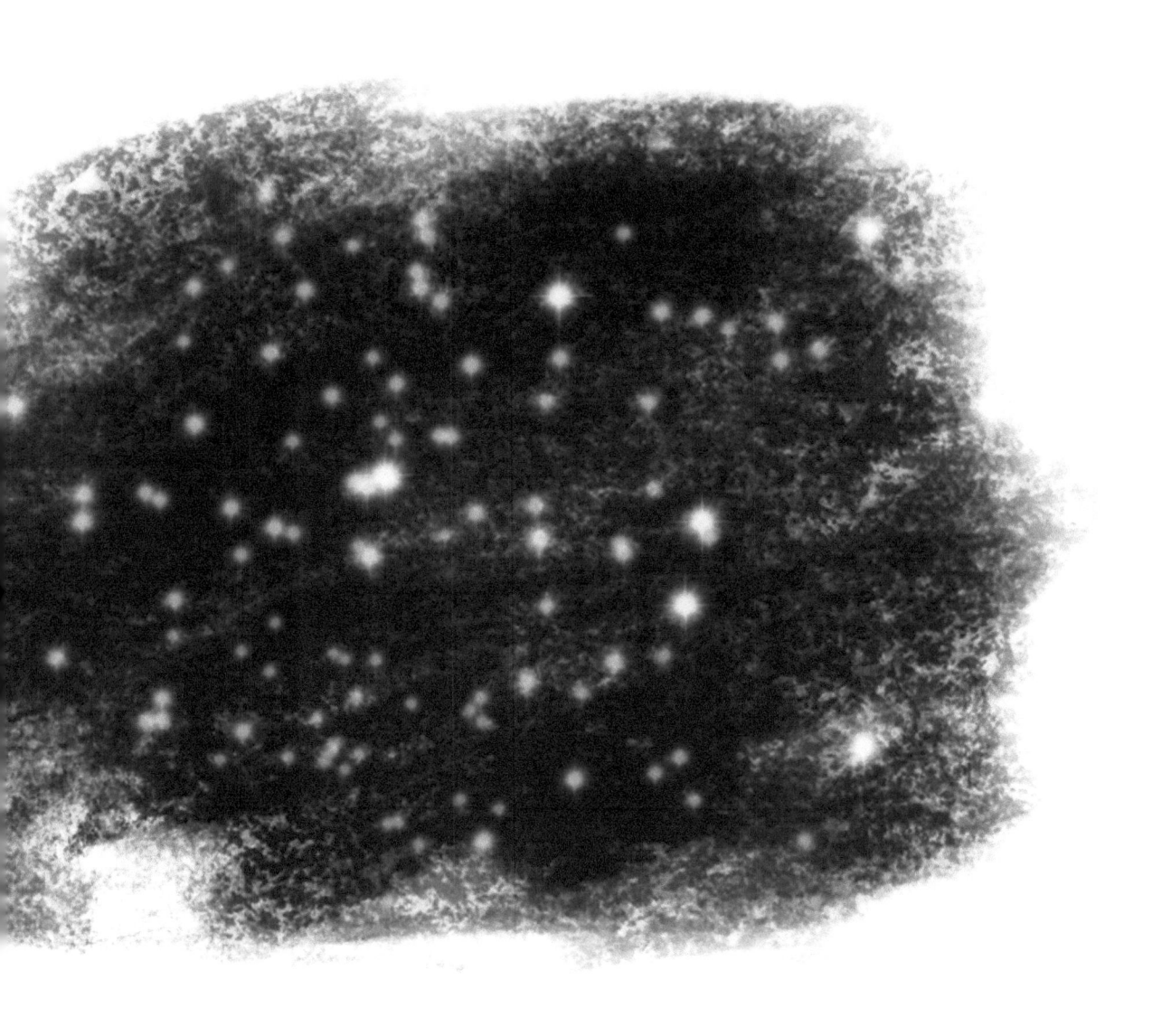

Invenio

About Team Friendship

In the year 2000, in a western suburb of Chicago, two bewildered high schoolers first crossed paths during an acting class lip-sync exercise of "Brush Up Your Shakespeare." They quickly became inseparable friends. From Jeremy doodling scenes of JJ battling Ninja Turtles at lunch, to inventing elaborate stories about pretend zoo trips during vampire invasions, the pair bonded over an instant, mutual love for the absurd. Thus, "Team Friendship" was born.

Now, 25 years later, the magic remains. They've stood by each other as best men in their weddings and have declared their children to be "Team Friendship 2.0." Their collaborative spirit has now bridged into writing and illustrating together.

They hope you enjoy this absurdity half as much as they've enjoyed creating it.

Printed in the USA
CPSIA information can be obtained
at www.ICGtesting.com
LVHW071131291124
797928LV00007B/177